Licking

J.V. Sadler

J.V. SADLER

Licking

J.V. Sadler

J.V. SADLER

J.V. Sadler's work has appeared in *Simple Simon Press, Last Exit Press,* and *Poetry Is Life Publishing*. Sadler earned a BA from Oberlin College and lives in Cincinnati, Ohio. This is Sadler's first collection.

You can reach the author on Facebook at www.facebook.com/JVSadlerAuthor.

Note to the Reader

Please be aware that *Licking* contains references to sexual assault, strong language, child endangerment and abuse, cannibalism, domestic violence, sexual content, blood and gore, suicide and self-harm, torture, kidnapping and imprisonment, and animal abuse.

Library of Congress Control Number: 2024900674

Paperback ISBN: 979-8-9896242-0-1

eBook ISBN: 979-8-9896242-1-8

Audiobook ISBN: 979-8-9896242-2-5

To those who helped me along the way.

CONTENTS

1. Introduction 1

2. New Baby Smell 3

3. The Decrepit Ones 4

4. The Baboon 16

5. Unafraid 18

6. Almost 25

7. Yappy 28

8. When the Walls Smile Back 40

9. How to Fix Yourself: A Guide to Improvement 41

10. And the Ground Cries 45

11. Hear from the Author of the Award-Winning Book: How to Fix Yourself: A Guide to Improvement 46

12. Family: Dinner 50

13. Growth, Spurt   63

14. Trapped, Chained   65

15. Your Neck Smells of Salt   87

16. Licking   88

17. I Licked You   114

INTRODUCTION

If you asked me, "Sadler, what is *Licking*?" I would look at you dumbfounded and shrug my shoulders. That's why developing a succinct synopsis for this piece of work was so difficult. I don't know what entered my mind during the creation of this book. I can say, however, that this book is an homage to the dreamscape . . . or the nightmare-scape. Many of these stories, such as "The Decrepit Ones" or "Yappy," came directly from my nightmares. I never intended to write my dreams down as short stories, but felt that it was disrespectful to my unconscious mind not to do anything with them. So, I started writing.

The ideas all came together after reading some of *5 Minutes to Success: Master the Craft of Writing* by Jeri Fay Maynard and D. W. Vogel. Maynard and Vogel suggest a "what-if" bubble map to help the creative process.

So, I got to work on my what-ifs and found that . . . geez . . . my ideas are messed up. And I love it!

I'm unsure when my love for the macabre started or when my interest in horror began. I'm a huge scaredy-cat, and I'm not a Halloween fanatic either. I respect the genre because it reveals something about ourselves and our society. What does our society consider as "scary?" How do our traumas, experiences, material conditions, etc., reflect what we fear most? These are a few of the questions I ask myself while writing in the genre.

My writing isn't straight-up horror. At least, I don't think it is. I describe it as "surreal" horror—bending the fabric of reality and adding a little pizzazz to it. A little razzle-dazzle. I'm not one for writing monsters or slasher killers. I'd rather explore everyday life—those dark thoughts that run through our heads. That's where I think the good stuff is.

This is *Licking*.

NEW BABY SMELL

she loves
   to pat its head
   but

   saliva oozes
   from her mouth
   twitches in her
   eye

   she might just
   eat,
   such tender meat
   smells so good

THE DECREPIT ONES

The Twain Children's Museum sign illuminates in the sunlight as a big, yellow school bus rolls in front of the building. Adults exit the buses first, then the little ones—holding hands, finding buddies, and carrying lunches. Heads are counted promptly. Trying to get the kindergarteners to stay still long enough to recheck the current headcount is difficult.

Men wearing shirts that read "Security" escort the class to the lobby: a group of Black and Brown kids led by pale, pinkish Caucasian men. One of the students, Kan, a quiet but much inquisitive Black boy, taps a chaperone on the side of the hip.

"Yes?" the smiling woman asks, wearing several lanyards around her neck.

"May I go to the bathroom?" Kan asks.

"You need to hold it," she says as they walk through the museum to where the tour begins—the dinosaurs.

Despite warnings to use "inside" voices, nice hands, and turtle paces, the children run, screaming toward the tyrannosaur that towers above everything in the middle of the showroom. A summer intern tells the tale of the great Cretaceous Period nearly seventy million years ago.

Some are unimpressed and veer to a much cooler stegosaur, while others are entranced that creatures as tall as the ceiling once roamed the Earth. But they fear the fated news that everyone understood to be common knowledge: the destruction of the dinos. The children's faces turn down in disappointment. Their smiles return after hearing the fun fact that dinosaurs do indeed still exist in the form of chickens and crocodiles.

Kan rubs his crotch a little. He has to go to the bathroom even worse but can hold it. In the distance, a wailing spirals down the halls like a lonely wind. It howls as if someone is crying for help. He ignores it and joins the group, heading toward the tour's next area.

The shadow of an Apollo rocket ship replica creeps upon them and a growing glee seems to race through everyone—both kids and adults. The black velvet rope does not prevent the tiny grabbing hands from feeling the rocket's metal and plastic exterior. Brimming with questions—especially about how the museum got

a huge rocket into the showroom—the children sur-
round the tour guide.

Kan glimpses the employees and wonders if they, too,
feel the same awe even though they see the exhibit daily.
This time, it is not a tour guide that speaks, but one
of the security. The escort, a white man with pepper
spray sticking out of his pocket, explains about the as-
tronauts, spacewalks, facts, and trivia.

Kan glances around the room, searching for the
chaperone whose hip he tugged. The woman with the
lanyards is nowhere to be seen. Yet that howling—*can
anyone else hear that*? the boy wonders—has become a
deep, mournful weeping.

The white security man leads the group to the bluest
room they've ever seen. As the children walk through
the blue tunnel, they learn about pufferfish. Then, a
substantial pixelated whale zooms overhead. Most of
the children believe the creature is real and, to them,
this has officially turned into the best field trip ever.
Kan notices that the security man's pepper spray has
miraculously transformed into a gun. And the weeping—*what is that*?

Somewhere down the hall, gibberish sounds deepen
into frightening snarls. The kids at the front of the
line cower. Their eyes swell with tears, and their noses

run snot. Some kids press their heels into the ground, stopping in their tracks. The white men reach into their pockets to reveal large, colorful lollipops. The kids wipe their faces and crowd around the men, reaching for candy. With lollipops in their mouths, the children pat their eyes dry, and the white men guide them further down the hall.

In the next exhibit, the children stare at wax figures whose hands also have thumbs and index fingers, nails, and curious lines going through the palms like railroad tracks on busy routes. They have reached the Dawn of Humanity. The wax figures of cave people are stuck in positions holding large clubs in the air or tackling coyotes.

The need to go to the bathroom overwhelms Kan, who searches for the lanyard-wearing chaperone. He doesn't see her anywhere. Mrs. Sarah, Ms. Jenkins, and their college assistants have also disappeared. But there are more white men; their guns are large. Kan taps a security guard on the elbow, who looks down at the boy with a stone face. Kan does not bother to ask for the bathroom.

And that crying! It has returned with growls weaved between. *Where is it coming from?* Kan tries to ignore the wailing—it is too worrisome to consider.

The children file through a set of double-mesh nets into the Jungle Room. Stuffed tigers and jaguars growl atop mâché rocks. An assortment of butterflies scurry in the air. The children nearly tackle one another while waiting in line to hold a butterfly. A bit of nectar is all it takes to entice a butterfly to land on a child's sweet finger.

Kan does not hold a butterfly. Instead, he counts the number of white men wearing bulletproof vests across their chests and backs with pads on their joints. Kan can no longer contain his bathroom urge, but is too afraid to poke the side of a tall weapon-wielding, angry-looking person. So, he crawls on the floor through the mesh nets.

Following signs and avoiding large men, Kan sneaks through the museum. He feels a tap on his shoulder and turns to see Fetty, a Black girl with big braids. She takes his hand, and they read the enormous foldable maps and signs until they reach a door with the word "toilet" pasted on its front. But, oh, they dare not go inside because from behind the door . . .

Weeping . . . Weeping . . .

A chill runs through the two; they break into a fast walk at a pace that does not seem out of place. They do not want a guard to catch them roaming around,

so they blend in with another group of kids too entranced by the tyrannosaur to notice. A timid white boy
with scraggly hair shakes uncontrollably. A look of fear
stretches across his face. Kan and Fetty approach the
boy.

"Are you okay?" Kan asks, gripping Fetty's hand.

The little boy furiously shakes his head.

"What's your name?"

"August," the boy whispers.

"What's wrong?" Kan asks.

Fetty points to the wet spot at the front of the timid
boy's pants.

"The bathroom," August whispers.

"Yes, we have to go too," Fetty adds.

"No. No. I saw inside," August says, his hands trembling.

In the bathroom, from where the crying leaks, the kids
starve. They feast on feces and drink their fluids. They
vomit from the smell and the thought. They are hungry,
so they eat that too. They are teens who have been
visitors for years.

In the bathroom, the kids starve. They sleep with
their heads in the urinals and their feet near the drains.

They obey the guards. They can *never* leave. They have to survive until they are eighteen—when they can be free. Starve till you're eighteen, and maybe one day, you can have your own children to starve.

"The kids . . . when I opened the door, they just stood there—dirty and smelly. They looked so sad." August focuses on the floor. "I've been here for three days hiding in the rocket ship. I'm hungry," he says.

Fetty shows her pockets. "I stole some snacks and juice boxes from the front desk."

The three snack on protein bars and slurp orange juice together, letting August have most of it. Kan shuffles as the urge to pee travels through his small body. He frantically scans the room and does a double-take at a fake elephant ear. He scurries toward the plastic plant and urinates behind it.

"We have to escape," August whimpers.

"We can't let the others go hungry!" Kan says with determination.

"I want to go home." August lets his tears flow.

"We'll get you home. Just help us save the others," Fetty says.

August nods and the three tiptoe to the front lobby and eye the desk.

"We need a map and more food," says Kan.

"I'll do it." Fetty skips to the desk.

"Hello, ma'am. May I have a map?" Fetty says to the woman whose scowl makes her face look like a prune.

"What happened to the map I just gave you?" the woman barks.

"Sorry, I lost it."

The woman mumbles, "Good for nothing brat."

While the woman rummages through a box, Fetty grabs handfuls of food and stuffs them in her skirt and training pants. All the kids knew Fetty still struggled with toilet training, but none teased her. It is the adults who always scold her.

The woman lifts a map from the box and pushes it into Fetty's hands. "Here. Don't lose it, okay?"

"Yes, ma'am," Fetty says with a smile. She skips her way back to August and Kan, who looks very impressed.

The three hurry through the exhibits to find their classmates. First, the dinos, then through space, the deep sea, cave dwellers, and the jungle. They walk through the maze of dollar-store foliage disguised as exotic jungle plants to another part of the museum. Toys, miniature trains, water games, and tower blocks crowd the room. Children scream with excitement and run around in circles. Armed guards watch as they play. One of the guards steps to the front and with a booming voice demands, "Time for the bathroom. Line up."

The class starts a line in front of the guard. Fetty, Kan, and August tap as many kids on the shoulder as they can in the brief amount of time they have. "Don't go to the bathroom. It's scary in there," the three whisper to those who will listen.

Only six out of the bunch of kids duck behind displays. Meanwhile, a new group of children enters the room to begin their playtime. August, Kan, Fetty, and the six escapees stay hidden. Together, they eat candy bars and devise the best escape plan a group of kindergartners can construct.

They blend in with the revolving groups of elementary and middle school-age children until they reach the front lobby again. Together, they try to push up against a heavy window. It will not open. Fetty grabs a metal chair, but she struggles with it. The surrounding children realize her intent and help her lift the chair and chuck it at the window. The glass shatters, the pea-sized shards flying away and sliding across the floor like marbles.

"Hey, get those kids!"

The children leap from the window while bullets whiz, but their small feet are too fast. They zig-zag to the parking lot like they've all seen in the movies. But the school bus has disappeared, and the parking lot is abandoned.

The children run as fast as they can toward anywhere. Somewhere unknown ahead of them, but away from the horrors behind. But they are not home-free. They have a mission to prepare. Once at their homes, the children gather weapons: kitchen knives, broomsticks without their heads, and pet dogs ready to charge. The children are surprised not to hear their parents object. In fact, *where are their parents*? There are none to be found.

Anywhere.

Not one grownup is available to help them—except for the guards. The guards—white men with big guns—always exist here.

Fetty snatches the car keys from the kitchen counter in her house. She has seen her parents drive before. She would sit on her mother's lap in the driver's seat and watch as the car moved and swayed down the roads.

The children are set and ready. Fetty is in the driver's seat. August holds a phone with a GPS program directing them. And Kan just stares out the window.

It is raining now. It is a lonely rain. A long rain. Every drop lasts a lifetime. Kan thinks about those kids in the bathroom. He and his accomplices must save the decrepit ones.

They must.

The car skips and spurts to the Twain Museum. The group of armed Black and Brown children and a little white boy named August opens the doors to the museum and runs inside, fearless and unwavering in their mission to save the others.

The guards' guns prove useless as their owners are so stunned they are unable to shoot. *Who has ever dared to fight back? Who is cocky enough to challenge their authority? This has never happened before. The children are fighting back. And winning!*

In the horrific bathroom, the decrepit ones wait on the other side of the door. Every day, the same. The ones who eat and drink filth. The ones who are scared. The ones shot for wanting food. Shot for wanting toys. Shot for wanting hugs. The survivors are the frail ones who live to grow old and will force their children to chew on muck one day.

But no more will they be oppressed. They will be saved now. Saved by the children who dared to fight back.

THE BABOON

The girls in the locker room snicker and scheme—their heads are low, and their smiles high. They laugh and giggle at jokes and anecdotes about her. The new girl. Today, she will be handled. At lunchtime, in the cafeteria, the girls see her carrying a poor man's lunch pail, probably filled with a poor man's meal: a ham and cheese sandwich, saltines, and a small bottle to refill with water from the fountain.

The girls prepare themselves. First, they storm and then crowd. The new girl looks around, confused and trembling. One girl knocks the lunch out of her hands, the pail hitting the ground with a disastrous *bang*. A thin object rolls across the floor from the pail.

Another girl pulls down the new girl's pants while another lifts the girl's shirt. The girl stands there, her C-cup bra exposed, her pubic hair curling from the coldness. Golden liquid runs down her legs. The boys ogle and grin. Pictures are taken.

They want to be entertained, the new girl thinks to herself. *They want a show.* Why else would they humiliate her so?

The new girl grabs the thin object that had rolled from the lunch pail across the foot-printed-tiled floor. The audience realizes it is penis shaped. A hard plastic thing—purple. She penetrates herself with it, but it has difficulty entering her body. The audience's amusement turns into disgust, then concern, then fear. The girl stands there, bent, forcing the plastic into her. Over and over. *This is what they want. They want a show.* There! Now, they could see all of her body. The outsides and the insides.

She screams a long, rippling scream. *This is what they want, right?*

Security forces her out, and they expel the new girl. She has become her own bully.

UNAFRAID

I repeat words of comfort to myself as I stare at my crumpled list. I look up at the festival gates, ready. *No matter what, keep going.* An October breeze blows as I put my hands through the arms of my sweater. My long hair tickles my nose as the wind pushes it in front of my face. The festival gates wait for me.

Walk.

Now.

The Festival of Fear haunted house howls my name. Growls and groans play through the speakers. I fear no werewolves, vampires, serial killers, or demented little girls holding creepy dollies. No, I am not afraid of those. But I *am* a woman who is terrified. I recheck my list, dreading each entry.

An attendant checks my wristband and beckons me to enter into the darkness. I hesitate, but my legs seem to move on their own. A hockey-masked man wielding

a large machete runs toward me. I jump and squeal at
the thrill. He gets close but dares not touch me. Next,
an angry butcher wearing a pig's face comes, stomping
his feet on the ground and thumping his arms against
his chest like a gorilla.

A couple behind me decide they've had enough and
exit through one of the emergency doors. The conse-
quences of leaving through that door? No refund.

The awaited terror arrives wearing a colorful wig,
big shoes, and a water-spray bow tie. The jolly clown
chuckles and smiles, his teeth bloody. My body freezes,
but my mind races. "No fear, no fear, no fear," I repeat.
My mumbles turn into screams. "No fear!"

The actor in the suit stops in his tracks. He looks
worried and reaches his hand out as if to comfort me.
I close my eyes tight. My hands hurt from my nails
digging into my palms. I can feel the eyes of seemingly
concerned patrons staring at me.

"Hey, do you need the emergency exit?" the actor
asks in a non-clown voice.

"No!" I respond with a shout.

I open my eyes to the clown's face. I see imperfec-
tions in his makeup, wrinkles, and shaven stubble. A
sudden realization comes to me. *Of course*! *He's just
a man. A man wearing makeup.* My breath steadies.

Then, I continue walking toward the end, completing the Festival of Fear haunted house. With a pen, I cross off the first entry on my list.

That night, I got my money back.

It is the next day, and my brown backpack rubs against my skin as I rock back and forth. My phone screen shines bright with colors and shapes from a matching game. I tuck the list I carry into the first zipped pocket of my backpack. I try to keep myself occupied. My leg bounces as if on its own, unable to quit. The other participants sit quietly. They are ready. I am not.

"Alright, everyone. Everyone set?" an overly smiley woman asks.

My rocking speeds up, as does my bouncing leg. A few people nod. The red exit sign looks inviting. But I must continue my mission. The smiling woman leads us to a large and official conference room.

Together, we watch demonstration videos: people falling in the air, slobber going everywhere. Clips of those who pulled their cords too early or too late only add to my concerns. Hands clap after the presentation; mine are still in my lap.

Changing into a bright-blue sky suit makes me feel like an astronaut or something, but I never want to go to space. I can barely cope with the sky. I ensure my list is safe before saying goodbye to my knapsack, and replacing it with a much heavier, bulkier bag stuffed with a parachute.

The outside is loud with the grinding engines of a small airplane. Before stepping into the craft, I close my eyes and pray. My golden crucifix is cold against my neck: a small token from Grandma before she died. I never go to church, but a little protection never hurts.

As the plane ascends, I keep my eyes on my feet, never looking out the windows. My breath is shallow and quick. An instructor taps me on the back and, with a warm smile, hands me a slender bag.

"Thank you," I utter, seconds before spitting and gagging into the bag.

He pats me on the back softly, comforting me.

"I'm sorry," I say.

He continues to pat my back. "No, it's alright. Been through this probably a thousand times," he says. "And you're not the only one." He points toward the back of the plane to a woman who is also holding a vomit-filled bag.

A second instructor repeats all the orientation beats before we reach the proper altitude. *This is it. There's no going back.*

The instructor stops his back rubs, clips his harness onto mine, and winks. "You ready?"

"No fear!" I shout.

We fall backward from the plane and into the free, open air. I keep my eyes closed tight. Whooshing whizzes past my ears. My skin flutters against the pressure. And I spin—too many times to count. The instructor yells something, but my head rings so loudly, I can't hear him. He yells again and motions with his hands. *Ah*! I understand and pull the red cord on my backpack. There is an immediate yank backward. My legs dangle beneath me and I am stumbling onto the ground before I can comprehend it. Once safely back on the ground, I retrieve my list from the first pocket of my backpack and cross off the second entry.

I've done it!

I've conquered the sky.

The next day, I'm on a swaying boat, whispering to myself, "No fear," as the waves slam against the wooden sides. My life jacket grips my body, and I bounce on my seat's wooden plank. My list is damp, and ink smudges on my thumb and wet fingers. I shiver against the sea's brittle air.

"Gear up!" a man wearing expensive diving gear yells.

I swing my legs and watch them hang off the side of the boat. When the diver isn't watching, I tinker with tubes and straps, hoping they will not do what they are meant to and praying the equipment will fail.

"Ready?"

We dive into the water. I flail first, sinking deeper and deeper. Fish tickle my swim fins. As I dive, I recollect my fears listed on the crumpled paper I had left lying on the boat's floor.

1. Coulrophobia—my fear of clowns.

2. Acrophobia—my fear of heights.

3. Thalassophobia—my fear of the ocean.

When my parents first brought me to the circus, they should've expected a toddler to scream and kick at the sight of a painted man with a red nose popping a balloon dog dead. From that day forward, I avoided all clown horror movies and dreaded the circus.

However, my fear of heights just showed up one day. I first realized I was afraid of heights after landing a job on the twenty-fourth floor of a skyscraper. I couldn't look out the windows, because the one time I did, I got so dizzy, I almost fainted. And the worry that the building would collapse kept me a nervous wreck.

My deep water fear started in sixth grade, after nearly drowning in the community swimming pool while playing Marco Polo in the deep end. After that, I couldn't go to the city aquarium without thrashing about. And the ocean? No way.

There is one fear, though that everyone seems to have. We try to escape it, but I decide to conquer it. Underwater, I shuffle around, going further down into the watery abyss. When deep enough, I push my mask and breathing tube from my face, and the costly gear sinks beneath me. Now, it is time to face the last fear on my list:

1. Thanatophobia—my fear of dying.

But I wish to die in triumph. Victorious.

No fear, I think one last time as water fills my mouth and nose. My body convulses and pulsates with each breath my lungs try to make. I wait for the great silence. When darkness envelops my vision, and nothing is left but ringing in my ears, I will have conquered all my fears. I have become a grim reaper and have done his job for him.

ALMOST

She lies flat on the ground, gurgling. Eyes closed, she is unaware of the small crowd watching over her, hesitant and unsure. The swimming pool is empty and the lifeguard is off duty.

"Is anyone a doctor?" asks Mr. Ferns, a neighborhood elder. He swims nearly every week during these hot summer days. Retirement treats him well, signified by his too-tight speedo and sounds of kids going "ew" at his saggy skin. He lives his life to the fullest.

Claire, a college student, asks, "Does anyone know CPR?"

The neighborhood librarian recalls books that mention CPR. "We can look up how to do CPR on our phones."

Folks nod their heads and whip out their devices.

Meanwhile, the woman's eyes roll back, the whites dominating and the irises disappearing.

"Who's gonna do it? I've seen CPR on TV before. Somebody's gotta do mouth-to-mouth," Claire says.

"I can't do it. I have herpes," says a teenage boy with a bursting sore on his top lip.

The librarian thinks. "I would need my lip balm. My lips are horribly chapped."

Mr. Ferns steps to the front. "I'll do it." He climbs his large body over the woman, and sits his bottom on her stomach.

Still unconscious, the woman spits up water.

Mr. Ferns glances at the librarian. "Tell me what to do."

The librarian kneels beside him and reads the first article on her phone. "Hi, everyone. My name is Jessica, and welcome to my blog. CPR stands for cardiopulmonary resuscitation."

Mr. Ferns looks at her in disbelief. "After that?"

The librarian scans her phone. "Okay, first put your hand in the middle of the chest like this." She demonstrates the position and continues. "Compress for at least 100 beats per minute."

"What's 100 beats per minute?"

"I dunno. Just count."

He presses against her chest, counting in his head silently. *One. Two. Three.*

"Faster." The librarian nudges Ferns, who loses the count in his head.

He starts over. *One. Two. Three.*

The woman on the ground stops gurgling, and a deadly quiet follows.

Thirty-five. Thirty-six. Ferns pauses. *Thirty-two? Thirty-two. Thirty-three.*

Under his body, she lies dead. The crowd seems unsure how to move forward.

"Should we have called an ambulance?"

YAPPY

I fiddle with my hands, waiting. The queue is short enough for me to get to work on time but long enough to converse with Rowland.

"What'd he say after that?" she asks, absorbed in my story.

"Well, he said he wanted to meet sometime," I reply, stepping forward as the line progresses.

"And?" Rowland leans forward.

"No! He has kids. I'm not ready to be a mother just yet."

"Ugh, too bad. He was cute too."

The guy I matched with on LUVer talked, looked, and seemed friendly. A man with kids, though? A big NO. I swipe through the list of men. One has a photo with both his hands around the waists of skinny women. Definitely NO. One man with a crooked smile catches my interest. I swipe, hoping that he'll match with me.

The line moves forward, and it is our turn to order. Rowland goes first. She always gets the sweet cappuccinos with extra sugar, extra caramel drizzle, and whipped cream. I'm next. I like my bitter Americanos with double espresso shots topped with black coffee.

The cashier smiles. She is pleasant, professional, and like a doll in an old-school diner waitress outfit. Our drinks are made quickly—a little too quickly. The receipt taped to the side of my cup is wet and blotted with inked words: Americano, DBLE. I took a sip. It is missing topped black coffee.

"Excuse me," I interrupt, getting the attention of a worker behind the counter.

A woman with a small green cap turns from her work. "Yes?"

I open my mouth. Muted burps jump out.

"Yes?" the woman asks again.

"I-uh-I—" I stutter at the start of my sentence. I try again. A stutter still. My hands sweat and my heart beats faster. My focus darts around the room, searching for Rowland, who puts her hand on my shoulder.

"Are you okay?"

My eyes go wide, but I say nothing. It's like a hand is around my throat, choking all the possible words. *My coffee is wrong*, I think to myself. *Topped black coffee.* But instead, I give up. "Everything's fine, sorry." I walk away, gripping my sad coffee; embarrassment and confusion overwhelm me.

Outside, the pavement scorches hot with heat waves rising from its surface. I slide and shuffle in my high heels and try to step directly on my foot patches. Rowland is smart. She wears nude flats with a golden ribbon on the front. I suppose once I'm in a higher position in the company, I too can wear flat shoes instead of high heels.

I glance at Rowland's heart-shaped face; envy is my first emotion. Some days, I wish I was her. But I'll never tell her that. Our friendship keeps me sane most days.

"Hey, what happened back there?" Rowland asks, facing me.

"I don't know," I say to her. *Why did that happen?*

We approach the brick FeVer building: Once a post office, it has become a business building for the marketing firm. It is large and threatening on a street of primarily small businesses that were once homes.

I gulp, taking the elevator to the fifteenth floor. Some people tighten their belts or bring a pair of sneakers to work to climb the stairs. Curiously, to go up several flights most of the time than to ride the jerking, wobbling machine.

I've traveled to every floor except the top five—Rowland works on the sixteenth. The fifteenth floor is the darkest in the building. The dim cubicles make the computer screens bright like small suns. I pretend the sound of the water cooler is the ocean.

I take two preemptive painkillers for the headache, which is bound to ensue by the end of the day. My desk is in a corner where I can see the entire floor. Everyone has their heads down in their work. No one speaks. Making friends among coworkers is a foreign concept. Fortunately, I knew Rowland before working at FeVer. She helped me get this position.

My phone rings—a familiar jingle. *A new match*! Jeffrey, age twenty-four. Just one year younger than me. The man with the crooked smile. I sit in my chair, and lean into my phone, nearly sucked into the enticing screen. He's tall with short auburn hair. His dimples light up his face, and his crow's feet eyes say he is joy embodied. *Should I message first*? *Or wait*? My mind volleys all the possibilities. The message cursor blinks as if impatiently waiting for me to type something. My hands dampen with sweat. *What would Rowland do*?

> Hey, how are you?

I type, not knowing what else to say. I turn back to my work. A few minutes later, the phone vibrates. *He's messaged back*!

> I'm doing fantastic. And you, beautiful?

He sends a smiling emoji that is warm and soft, not suggestive or pushy. He is the first man on the app to call me beautiful. Not pretty, sexy, or cute. Beautiful.

The laptop at my desk sits, expecting some progress. My eyes switch between screens, traversing the brewing romance on my phone and slugging through work on a blank computer. I pause at one particular message.

> This Saturday is a poetry open mic. Wanna go?

My heart races. A minute can't pass before I reply with an enthusiastic,

> Yes!

I crack my knuckles to continue texting. Team leader Josh steps in my direction. He has a soft, young face and dark slicked-back hair. Despite being the least experienced in the group, he is the team leader.

"Jaina. Meeting."

I stand, adjust my skirt, and follow him to a conference room. Our manager looms at the end of the table, a general to his small army.

"Please sit," the manager says.

It was me, him, and team leader Josh. My feet sweat and slide again in my heels. This meeting can go one of two ways: I'm either a superb worker or a soon-to-be ex-employee. The seat prepared for me is faux leather—uncomfortable and worn.

"Yes?" I ask.

"Josh says you've been on your phone a lot recently. Just reminding you that you shouldn't be texting at work."

"Yes, sir," I utter.

"We have a deadline approaching," he continues. "I'll need you to come in this Saturday." My manager folds his arms, and Josh turns to me with a puppy dog face. "Any questions?"

I open my mouth but offer no objection. I push, straining my body to talk. My face goes red.

"Jaina, you alright?" Josh asks, looking at my face.

Damn. "Yes" is all I have strength for. I return to my desk. *That meeting could have been an email.*

I text Jeffrey.

Can we reschedule?

He understands, and my nerves calm. We decide on a restaurant which I look forward to, though I dread having to work on Saturday.

Every few seconds, I force myself to open my eyes. I glance at my pencil skirt and frilly blouse. Both are wrinkled. My hair is twisted into a messy bun, but un-like those cute styles. This bun is calling for help.

I think back to Jeffrey. He and I were on the phone together all night. His deep, raspy, but sweet voice cooed me to sleep. I woke up this morning with his snores in my ear on the phone. Rowland tells me she was called in for Saturday, too—a surprise. Usually, the bot-tom-of-the-barrel employees get called in to work Sat-urdays.

My phone is silent—turned off. I have a strong urge to open LUVer and remove myself from the monoto-nous hell of my job on a Saturday.

Someone taps me on the shoulder, and I jump. Josh stands behind me, eager and sprite. "Jaina. Meeting."

I follow him to the elevator and ask, "What floor?"

"Twenty."

Did he just say twenty? "What floor?" I ask again.

"Twentieth."

This is real! I've never been past floor fifteen. The important people, the top-level people, are up there. *Am I being called upstairs for a raise or, better yet, a promotion?*

On floor twenty, we walk to what seems to be the largest conference room in the building. The room is pristine, with windows expanding from floor to ceiling. Oversized padded rolling chairs are arranged around the room. Out the window, I see other skyscrapers, including our rival company, Lavender. There's the city bridge over the river and even the little cafe where Rowland and I get our morning coffees.

Rowland and a few others are here as well. Everyone takes their seats and waits for directions. A tall, slender man wearing a shoulder-padded, navy blue suit walks in. The color blue establishes he has power. He is *the* Chris Staples, my boss's boss.

"Thank you, everyone, for coming in this Saturday." His voice has a southern twang.

I turn my head and see Josh sweating.

"I would like to announce that we are merging with Lavender."

Everyone gasps. Murmurs fill the room. He goes on about stats and dull technicalities. I prop my chin up with my hand, my elbow resting on the table. I assume the meeting is over because people stand and begin leaving.

As I near the exit, Staples clears his throat. "Excuse me."

I turn my head to meet Staples's eyes.

"What's your name?" he asks.

"Uh, Jaina," I say, sitting back down. Josh lingers in the room. As the door swings shut, I see Rowland in the hall, waiting for me.

"I've been looking at progress reports and . . ."

A smile creeps onto my face.

"We're gonna have to let you go."

My smile dissolves. I open my mouth to protest, but I cannot speak. I muster the strength to shake my head. *I am a diligent, exemplary employee.*

"With this new merger, we had to make some hard decisions."

I stand and furiously shake my head. Unintelligible sounds come from my throat. *This is unfair!*

Josh steps in. "Jaina, it's time to go."

Josh reaches for my hand, but I swat his away. Unable to speak, I continue shaking my head as that's the only way to express my dissatisfaction.

"Jaina, please," says Staples, stepping closer.

An expensive, shiny pen sits on the table. I reach for it, throw it at Staples, and slam my fists on the table.

"Uh-uh-uh," I utter.

"Don't make me call security," Josh says, nervousness lines his words.

"Uh-uh-uh." I storm out the door.

Rowland is there smiling. "So?"

Collapsing into her arms, I am in tears. "Uh-uh-uh."

Sunday is the day I forget my worries. Jeffrey and I will fall in love on Sunday, melt into one another, and pretend Monday doesn't exist. My feet usually hurt as I walk the pavement, but today, I wear flats to compliment my flowing summer dress. The LUVer app notification appears on my screen. Jeffrey sent a message five minutes ago.

> I got us a seat near the front, to
> the left.

I trot faster and eventually arrive at my destination: an Italian restaurant. The relationship blogs I read said

never to order the spaghetti and meatballs—my favorite—as it can be an "uncomplimentary" dish.

When I open the doors to the restaurant, I see him
and his crooked smile. He towers over me when he
stands and opens his arms. We embrace, his soft skin
touching mine. We could be lovers. We could be a lot
of things to one another. He notices my flushed face
and grins wider. I return his smile and we hug again.
He pushes my chair in as I sit, then takes his chair and
moves it closer.

"How are you today?"

He sounds better than on the phone. Deeper. My
outdated cell could not do his voice justice.

I blush and say, "Fine. And you?"

"Fine." He chuckles."Been here before?"

I shake my head.

We trade anecdotes, cackling at each other's jokes
and not caring about anyone around us. He convinces
me to get the spaghetti and meatballs. My heart does a
quick hopscotch when he takes my hand into his, and I
feel like a young girl again.

"Wanna get outta here?" he asks.

But doubt invades. Maybe this is too good to be
true. Maybe this is going too fast. Something in my gut

tells me this is wrong, but I ignore the signs. I think to myself, *What would Rowland do*? "Sure," I say softly.

His home is clean, quaint, and simple. I sat on the couch and put my hands in my lap, not knowing what to do with myself.

"Want some wine?"

It's happening again. I can't speak. I shake my head. He sits beside me and leans as if expecting me to kiss him. *No.*

He is impatient and takes it, anyway. I push him, opening my mouth to say no, but I can only make muffled sounds.

"I really like you," he says, kissing me.

I bite down hard on his tongue, and his once-soft face turns hot with anger. He pushes me down on the couch and climbs on top of me.

"Uh-uh-uh." It's all I can say through the night as he forces himself on me. I cannot speak. I cannot scream. No one hears my pleas for help because they do not exist. I am tongue-tied, mouth-twisted, a halfway mute—reduced to a plaything for the world to do as it wants.

WHEN THE WALLS SMILE BACK

The walls flicker like a camera's lens—piercing neon yellow slices through the darkness.

"$Wh_o\ a_r^e\ y_o{}^u$?" the room utters. "$W_h{}^o\ a^r{}_e\ y^o{}_u$?" It repeats with a sing-song inflection.

A buzzing in the air spirals into your ear. No, it's a hiss—a venomous *shrill*.

The room closes in, and the demon brandishes its razor teeth.

You be sure to tell it your name.

HOW TO FIX YOURSELF: A GUIDE TO IMPROVEMENT

When you find yourself stuck, crying alone at night, open this book, and you will find yourself again. But first, cry. Cry out the pain—all of it. Cry out the suffering. Hold your breath until you can't anymore, then inhale. Now, exhale! Blow it out, cough it out, spit it out. Do what you have to do to get that devil out of you.

You're reading this because there is a *devil* inside of you that you can't seem to shake. But don't fret. Fortunately, I can show you how to kick the gloom and return to your normal self.

Step 1: Visualize yourself standing in a circle. With you are the things you enjoy, people you love, spirit, health, wealth, etc. All those things you've ever needed or wanted. Outside this circle is the mess: the divorce, the drama, self-deprecation, negativity, judgment, and all the rest of the horror.

Step 2: Imagine the ugliness inside of you. Breathe it out. *It's breathing down your neck*. Exhale it out of the circle, because only greatness lies in this circle.

Step 3: Next, visualize all that ugliness shuffling itself outside your circle and transforming into a figure standing before you. *Eyes glaring green, staring ... staring ...* This shadowy figure is nothing but gloom and represents everything wrong in your life.

Step 4: Unsheathe your imaginary sword. Cut down the gloom. *It is strong*. Cut it up, cut it out, *cut it off*. But remember, do not step out of the circle.

Step 5: You are the winner! You are victorious. Remember these facts, and you will be fine. *It wants you.* But do not step out of the circle—no, not even your pinky toe. Wait. Your heel!

Step 6: Why did you back up? *Step closer.* You are fearless, remember? But your heel, oh God.

Step 7: *You are its plaything.* Do not panic. Show no fear. You are in charge here. Wipe your cheeks and get tissue for your runny mascara. You'll be just fine. Just do as I say.

Step 8: The shadowy figure encompasses the room now. It is in the circle with you. *It licks the sweat from your neck.* Do not listen to its whispers. Think positive thoughts only.

<u>Step 9</u>: Scream for help. No, do not leave the circle! That will make it worse. Scream for help. Scream!

<u>Step 10</u>:

AND THE GROUND CRIES

With each step you take, the ground moans and wails. Its mouth is wide open like a babe looking for a tit. Careful, now. Tiptoe you must. One wrong step, and you'll slide down its tongue, get chewed on by rattling teeth, and swallowed in pieces. Down to the abyss, into its belly, you slip. The demon—your darkness—wants you. Careful, now. You'll be digested like pizza on a Friday night.

HEAR FROM THE AUTHOR OF THE AWARD-WINNING BOOK: HOW TO FIX YOURSELF: A GUIDE TO IMPROVEMENT

A crackling loud voice from the speakers monotonously announces, "Now presenting the award-winning author of *How to Fix Yourself*, Avery Means."

Avery, a tiny woman from Calabasas, California, struts confidently onto the stage. She lifts her hand into a beauty pageant wave. Her bright smile lightens the room. The audience is on their feet, and their clapping seems endless. Avery puts her hand up and the audience takes their seats, eager to listen and learn.

The stage lights beam down onto her forehead and blinds her. Her body heats up with the residual effects of excitement and nervousness.

A sudden hush fills the room when she stands in the middle of the stage, strong and power-filled. Not even a cough or slight shuffling can be heard. It is silent. Avery takes a moment to gather herself, a moment that is too long and drawn.

"Hi there, superstar! My name is Avery Means. I am a thirty-two-year-old single mom from Calabasas, California. All my life, I avoided mirrors. I didn't want to confront my ugliness. My insecurities. I couldn't even do my makeup!"

The front row leans closer.

"*How to Fix Yourself* is not about perfection. Instead, it teaches that you are redeemable and fixable."

Heads nod in agreement.

The lights on the stage shine brighter and hotter on her skin. Avery looks up, hoping to signal the tech crew.

"We are all redeemable. But first, we must acknowledge the *devil* that exists within every one of us."

The audience can no longer be seen behind the falling dust of the stage lights. Lights have swallowed them, even so, Avery feels their presence. She steps back, her heel hitting hard against the wooden floor. She steals a sneaky glance to the left and right and sees crew members backstage. They are entranced, gripping their clipboards like precious artifacts.

"Everyone, I'd like you all to do an exercise with me. First, imagine this entire audience, this entire building, is inside a large circle. That's a huge circle!"

The audience chuckles dryly.

"Inside this circle is energy—our positive energy. Outside this circle are all of your fears. Now, hold your breath."

People puff their cheeks and hold air inside. Per the speaker's directions, they inhale. Then, with a big huff, they exhale everything. Loud, exaggerated exhalations whiz through the auditorium. Satisfied with the exercise, Avery glances at the backstage crew. They no longer hold their clipboards. Their arms are stiff to their sides, and they stare with bright neon green eyes.

"Good, uh, job," she says, trembling at the sight of the neon eyes. The darkness is here.

A large, narrow bag sits at the edge of the stage. Avery approaches the bag, pulls out a cloth, and uses it to wipe the sweat ruining the collar of her expensive shirt. She reaches into the bag again, pulling out a long sword. Avery closes her eyes and does the breathing exercise again. When she opens her eyes, the stage-right crew has disappeared. The stage-left crew are now unmoving shadow figures.

It is here.

She unsheathes her sword and points the tip toward the audience. "The next step is to remember that you have already . . ." She trails her words. ". . . You have already won."

The audience stands as if the crowd is one. Their eyes are now neon green and staring forward in a trance.

"I have already won," she whispers to herself, wavering.

The shadowy figures are now onstage, approaching her circle. She can feel them scanning her. She can feel their thick breaths on her neck.

"Positive thoughts only," Avery yells, trembling. She sweats profusely, yet her mouth is bone dry.

You are mine.

The audience applauds, clapping their hands, listening to the sound of ripping flesh, and watching as she screams.

FAMILY: DINNER

"See, you have to discipline your wife."

The dinner guests listened to the old man at the head of the table. Grandpa—he was always served first. Grandma April fiddled in the kitchen, ensuring the plating would attract his eye. Her hands shook as she set the silverware on the neatly made plate. *Lasagna. Don't fail me now.*

She returned from the kitchen with a plate full of food. After placing the plate in front of her husband, April scanned the faces of the guests. Tears brimmed on her daughter May's lower eyelids as she sat by her husband. Her son-in-law nodded his head as Grandpa continued. March's lips were pursed closed. Reggie and Steve's faces were red hot, but still, they were silent. And Sul looked around as if preparing to say something.

"The weather said it might snow later on. I could almost see reindeer flying in the sky." Sul chuckled.

The guests remained solid-faced.

"See, if I were you," Grandpa said, "I wouldn't let any woman tell me what to do. April? She wouldn't dare."

At that moment, April's hand slipped, causing a full glass of water to spill into his lap. The already quiet guests hushed into a dead silence.

"Woman!" He gripped her arm. Hard.

She saw the furious gaze in his eyes. *Please, not in front of company*, April's eyes seemed to plead.

His grip tightened. *Was he going to swing?* She closed her eyes as if waiting, but she felt the grip release. He let her go . . . *this time*, she thought.

"I'll get you a towel," she said, entering the kitchen to retrieve paper towels for the mess.

"See, you have to train your women," Grandma April heard her husband say sternly.

As she returned from the kitchen, April tried to cover the red mark on her arm with the sleeve of her shirt, but she knew everyone could see.

Her son-in-law mumbled "Mmm" in agreement as April cleaned up Grandpa.

"Mom?" May asked with a concerned tone.

Grandpa slammed his fist on the table, making everyone jump. "Shut it!"

April shot a quick scowl at her. *Don't; you'll just make things worse.*

But it was obvious to all that her anniversary was ruined.

It was Christmas Eve, and April held the tin dish tight, her hand shaking and her feet weak. On the tin sat a glass of water, a shot of whiskey, steak, potatoes, and condiments. She entered the gloom-lit, violet-brown room and faced her husband.

His face was more wrinkled than hers and in a permanent scowl. He wore thin wire glasses to help his small, almond eyes see far away. She set the dish on a round oak table before him and waited for his reaction as he took his first bite. He chomped on the potatoes but kept his face like eroded stone. *The whiskey helps with digestion.*

Next, the steak. He cut into the meat. Right away, he tossed his fork and knife across the room. After balling up his napkin, he threw it in April's face. The tin he pushed away, the dishes jingling and teeter-tottering on top.

Why me? April thought to herself. She inhaled, took the plates away, and returned to the kitchen.

She had bought three cuts of sirloin for dinner-time. The sound of the plastic wrap of the second steak ripped through the kitchen, accompanied by soft sniffles and watery eyes. The thermometer sticking out of the sizzling meat read 135 degrees Fahrenheit. After thirty minutes, she placed the food on their dishes and tiptoed to the dining room.

"Took you long enough."

April presented the food again: a newly filled glass of water and another whiskey shot, steak, potatoes, and condiments. He ate the potatoes again, fast. Then, he took a swig of the whiskey and the water. Eventually, he cut the steak right down the middle.

April's heart dropped to the burgundy carpeted floor. The man took off his glasses and stood. April's mind told her to brace for impact.

But when the hand swung, her body did something. *No more*!

Her hand came up to meet his, stopping his slap. She plunged the steak knife into his shoulder with the strength of a woman who'd had enough.

She didn't know why this night differed from the countless others nor how she acquired the courage to do what she did. Perhaps she was just a tired woman. Survival is indeed a finicky thing. April ran for the phone and dialed her daughter. "May, I need your help." Christmas was ruined.

April and May were in the kitchen mixing cocktails.

"I hope it doesn't rain on them," said April, looking through the window at the gray clouds forming. The moon shone through the window onto her face, making her skin seem misty white.

"They'll be fine, Mom," May replied, sipping her concoction. Her face, wrinkled and sunken, still showed that alcoholic, midlife-crisis, white woman glee—that carefree, "I-rule-the-world" glee.

A ring of the doorbell interrupted their conversation. May exited the kitchen to greet the visitors while April stayed behind, checking on the almost-done casserole.

"My babies!" she heard May saying.

A sound of footsteps headed toward the kitchen. March and Sul stood in the doorway with grand smiles and arms wide.

"Grandma!" they said in unison.

"Well, go take your seats. I'll be out in a minute," April said, opening the oven to check on the boiling casserole. *This will be good*, she thought to herself. *My best work yet*. April stared at the casserole through the oven glass and smiled.

Ding!

The oven timer sounded. April grabbed her mittens and took the heavy dish out. "It's hot! It's hot!" The bean casserole spilled over the sides as she entered the dining room "May, make room on the table. I made a casserole, everyone," Grandma said.

Grandma was pleased to see all eyes ogling the dish; they were ready to rip it to shreds.

Sul reached for the silverware.

Slap!

He pulled back his hand.

April gave him *that* look. "Don't eat until everyone is here."

A knock sounded, followed by the doorbell. April motioned for May to answer the door.

"May!" Uncle Reg's voice boomed through the home. May and Reggie embraced each other for a long moment. "How's my baby sis?" Reg asked.

"Holding it together," May replied.

Uncle Stevens joined in on their embrace. "You don't need that asshole."

May nodded and smiled. The three of them took their seats at the table. April was glad that May and her husband had split. He was certainly an asshole.

Everyone smiled and rubbed hands, preparing for dinner.

"Hey, where's Grandpa?" Sul asked, scanning the table.

"We will serve him soon." Grandma waved her hand above the casserole to cool it down and prevent the contents from boiling over. "Get up and say grace." She gestured toward Sul who was fiddling with his silver-ware.

He stood too proud and cracked his knuckles loud-ly. Stevens massaged his forehead, Reg leaned in, and March rolled her eyes—all at the performance bound to ensue.

"Well," he started incorrectly already. "Lord." He closed his eyes and stumbled through every word. "You are our shepherd, and we shall not want."

Everyone seemed to doze off, concentrating only on the dinner. After Sul's poor prayer attempt, the table ended with an "Amen."

Dinner was ready. Plates and silverware clinked. The table was filled with steaming food: Mashed pota-toes with gravy, corn on the cob, spinach and artichoke stuffed portobello mushrooms, sizzling glazed pork, lemon cake, chocolate cake, and Grandma's special bean casserole.

Grandma April took her seat, satisfied at the sight, except for her granddaughter March who frowned and squinted hard at the dinner table.

"So, you all know why I gathered you all here." May took a deep breath.

April, face downturned, put her hand on her daughter's back to console her. She blamed herself for the pattern of relationships that had transpired. Grandpa always said he believed in "disciplining your wife." He would respond with a swift slap to April's face upon the slightest inconvenience. Those nights, May seldom talked. She stayed up as a little girl in her brothers' bedroom, holding tight as she heard items thrown in the next room. Reg, Stevens, and May—the three would play games together: *Space Invaders* was their favorite.

May had been married to someone not as bad as Grandpa but bad enough. Her relationship with her brothers and mother helped. Those four would call back and forth through the odd hours of the night, giving comforting words to one another.

May's ex-husband didn't hit her like Grandpa hit Grandma, but he might as well have stabbed her in the heart with a rusty knife. And every time May caught him with another woman, they would talk, he would say some pretty words, they'd kiss, make love, and the smiles would return . . . until he was caught again with another woman. May stayed up late, getting drunk off her ass, crying about how she wasn't a good enough woman. The final insult was that May caught her husband with her cousin on Grandma's loveseat. May hit rock bottom, then said, "Enough." She wasn't going to suffer as her mother had.

"Thank you all for being here for me." May's voice broke as she continued. "There were some days when I thought, you know, life wasn't worth it anymore. Being betrayed repeatedly by someone who was supposed to love me." She paused, wanting to say something more, but the words never came.

Grandma interrupted the silence. "How's the food, everyone?"

Everyone approved simultaneously, with pats on the bellies and thumbs up.

"The bean casserole tastes a little different. What did you make it with this time?" Stevens inquired.

Grandma put her finger to her lips. May glanced at her with a smile of contentment and nodded her head.

While the family ate, Sul and the uncles talked loudly about outdoor sports. April listened to them, laughing at their jokes and enjoying the moment.

March asked with a harsh tone, "Is Grandpa coming?"

The table turned to April.

"Oh, he's upstairs taking a rest. His new medication makes him sleepy. Don't bother him," she replied.

"I'll go get him." Sul lifted himself from the table and headed for the steps.

"Don't bother him," Grandma April muttered, her voice stronger.

Sul was already up the stairs. And even though he heard Grandma, he knocked on the door.

No response.

He cracked open the door and poked his head through the opening. It was dark in the bedroom, but he could see that the bed sheets were disheveled. He tiptoed to the bed and said, "Grandpa."

No response.

Uncovering the bed in one motion, Sul was surprised that the bed was empty.

"Sul, come downstairs."

Startled by his grandmother's voice in the doorway, Sul's nerves left his body and he obeyed, still wondering where Grandpa was.

"How is he?" Uncle Reg asked.

"Uh . . ."

"Don't worry about him. Let's eat," April interjected.

The family continued eating.

March's utensils clinked loudly against her plate. "So," March started, "How're you and Grandpa?" She let out a disgusted sound somewhere between a *ugh* and a *yuck*.

Grandma stayed silent.

March let go of her silverware, letting it drop to the table. *It begins.* "Can we all stop pretending?" March finally let out.

"March!" May intervened.

"You're a lonely, pathetic woman who let terrible people into our lives," March said.

"I am a survivor!" Grandma stood.

May stood tall at the table with Grandma and yelled, "Enough."

The table quieted down.

April breathed a long breath, then said, "It's Grandpa," and wiped her running nose.

A terrible, confused silence traveled through the room.

"The casserole. It's Grandpa."

"What?" March asked, still very confused.

"I cooked Grandpa," April said, wheezing. "I skinned him. I cut him up. I seasoned him. Then, I baked him. Grandpa is in the bean casserole."

Sul vomited up his dinner. March stared at the casserole, horrified and in shock.

"*What*?" March asked again.

"Jesus Christ," Stevens uttered as Reg stopped himself from gagging.

April sat down. "Your mother and I planned it."

Everyone turned their heads toward an expressionless May.

"We were tired of men mistreating us. My mom was beaten for years. And me? Cheated on constantly." May wiped tears from her eyes.

April left for the kitchen and returned with a large frozen bag filled with parts. Some fingers, other pieces of arms. After seeing her grandfather's wedding band through the mangled body pieces, March vomited next to Sul's puddle.

"We are survivors." Grandma held her daughter's hand. "Your grandfather always complained about my cooking. Not enough of this. Not enough of that. Well, we made him useful for once. We got tired of serving him, so we *served* him. Isn't he delicious?"

March wiped her mouth. Sul picked up his phone, but Stevens grabbed his hand and took the phone from his grip.

"What the hell?" Sul said. His mouth dropped.

"That's still my sister," Stevens said, breaking the phone against the wall.

Reg stepped on it, making sure the cell phone was crushed. "We handle this as a family."

No one else dared reach for their phones.

"Everyone sit," April demanded. No one moved. "I said sit!"

They all took their seats.

"Let's finish our family dinner."

Through the night, they pieced through the meal, ensuring to compliment the chefs. May leaned over to her mother and whispered, "I have a recipe planned for my ex-husband."

GROWTH, SPURT

There are branches,
   bursting from your lungs

   Seeds planted mature
   into a foliage beast

   Cough and
   spit

   brown, soggy, saliva-painted
   Autumn leaves,

   twigs cut
   into your intestines

   There is
   a large tree

It grows inside you
Give it nutrients

TRAPPED, CHAINED

Oswald eats his breakfast—three eggs sunny-side up, toast, and a biscuit—painstakingly slow. He tiptoes through the meal, meticulously taking each bite, chewing into a bolus, and swallowing carefully. His napkin is folded the way he likes it. He wipes his mouth and then properly re-folds the cloth. After finishing his meal, the dishes are washed. Not a plate or fork is left for tomorrow.

The table is wiped clean. And the chair, which he pushes in, ensuring not to scrape it against the floor. *Always pick it up gently.* The sound of someone fiddling with the mailbox interrupts his morning routine. He retrieves the mail while waving hello to the mailman, who now makes his way to the next home. *He's nice. Real nice.*

He shuffles through his mail and throws the unpaid bills into the trash. He reads through the advertisements from companies he's never heard of: low-interest credit cards, car insurance, charities, magazines, and catalogs. Once he finishes browsing, he unlocks a door that welcomes steps down to the basement. He descends and does not return until hours pass.

The following day, the mailman stuffs more envelopes in the mailbox. This time, Oswald cannot ignore the letters. *Damn.* Again, his morning is ruined by notices and ordinances. The papers say he has sixty days to leave. The lights are to be cut off sooner than that. Overdrafted bank accounts threaten revenge. His lifestyle, foiled by debt and the American economic system, is to end.

Snapping the wrist of his black latex gloves, he prepares himself for a mess. His knife is extra sharp today. He blows out air from his puffed cheeks and opens the door to the basement. He does not return until sunrise.

Today's breakfast is three eggs and a strawberry muffin: a last meal in Oswald's twentieth-century kitchen. Pieces of red peek from the mass of sweet brown—a conglomerate of "bready" tastiness. Bags sit in the living room, waiting to be carried along. The walls are blank with the dusty outlines of photos and paintings that once decorated the room. A large packing truck hums in the driveway, holding what few pieces of furniture Oswald did not sell. Before leaving, he takes one final look down the basement steps.

"Goodbye, boys," he whispers in the bleak air.

Downstairs, a man chained to the concrete walls in the basement cannot hear the vehicle roll away. Krin, still high from whatever concoctions Oswald gave him yesterday, slowly cracks open his eyes. He lies, sprawled, wearing good-smelling clothes. He notices that his arms are free of dirt and grime. Sniffing at his armpits, he thinks to himself, *I am clean*. But it is something else that he is feeling—an odd sort of lightness. Something is off.

He is chained by his left wrist with his right hand free to wander. Across from him, a slumped Paul drools from the corner of his mouth. Paul, Krin recalls, had *two* legs before Oswald put the men to sleep. Krin turns to glance at his own legs.

"Paul!" Krin yells. His throat ripples and hurts with each shout. "Oh my God, my legs!" Krin touches the stump of a knee that had a shin, calf, ankle, and foot attached yesterday. "Paul!" Krin whimpers as he sees both legs look the same.

He ugly cries as Paul, inebriated, slowly regains his vision.

Paul barely recognizes Krin crying and flailing. *What's he going on about now?*

Krin points at Paul's legs.

Paul glances head down, then at his friend, whose body flips and flaps like a land-trapped fish. Paul cries "Oswald!" and Krin gags loudly.

The sounds of the men hyperventilating fill the room. They face the realization that they will never have the ability to *walk* out of this place. Yet, Oswald had left them a gift. Fleshy appendages lay next to them both. Oswald knew they would miss their appendages and returned them. Their legs lay teasing them . . . forever useless.

Two vats—one filled with grain, the other with fresh water—are within arm's reach. Krin finds the gesture suspicious. Oswald always brought their meals to them and watched as they ate. He'd stare, sometimes panting, sometimes touching their lips. If they bit, they'd be welcomed with a quick punch to the nose and no meal for the rest of the day.

The two chained men cry, writhe, and moan for a while, holding their strewn limbs. They yell for Oswald but he never comes. When they finish their screaming tirade, they lie back down to sleep. What else can they do? And they sleep for hours.

Day One

The two men play their game of "night or day." Paul guesses day and Krin night. If Oswald comes down the steps with eggs and ham, it's day. If he comes with mashed potatoes and fried chicken, it's night. Both lost if he came with Reuben on sourdough or turkey on rye—that meant it was afternoon.

But food does not come. They wait but are impatient. Stomachs rumble. Mouths are dry For Oswald to break his pattern is unusual.

Krin glances at their waste bucket, which stinks horribly from sloshy, old excrement and urine. "Oswald!" Krin yells. "Oswald, we're hungry."

Nothing.

"Oswald! What's the news?" Krin calls loudly.

Still touching his stitched knees, Paul groans. He admires, in a helpless way, the cosmetic job done. The spot is still numb, giving him that odd sensation of the area being more extensive than it is. It is like the sensation after getting a shot of local anesthetic at the dentist. For one tooth, half the face can get numb.

"Oswald!"

"Hey, man," Paul interrupts. "Give it up." He gestures toward the remnants of his legs. "Look at what he did to us."

They throw their loose limbs as far away as they can. In a few hours, the legs will deteriorate, which will be another horrible odor they will have to endure until Oswald comes to clean up.

But he does not come.

They sit in silence, boredom, and annoyance. A dingy light keeps them company, and they watch as rats scramble around them. From the corners of the room, crawling insects come in endless numbers. What were they to do without their captor?

Splash! Krin slams his free hand into the vat of water. He does it again. This time water splashes onto his chained friend.

"Watch it," Paul says, slightly entertained.

Krin lifts his wet hand.

A third splash ensues, but this time from Paul. The two men giggle like girls playing in a park sandbox. They are amused by nothing nowadays, having spent a month chained in the basement of Oswald's humble home.

Oswald is neither a psychopath nor a sociopath either. The results of the behavioral tests the psychiatrist did were normal. He's a typical Caucasian man, perhaps making him most dangerous. He weaves through society without anyone ever doubting his character, his actions, his mind. He could have relationships, go out with friends, and get a good job—although not good enough to sustain his eccentric lifestyle. He never knew how expensive caring for the two men would be.

He tried his best to mother them. He chose grown adults because he couldn't stand to hurt a child. He would have washed them more if they had stopped fighting and biting. That's the only time he hits them.

Unbeknownst to the men, Oswald cried the day he kidnapped them and chained them in his basement. He knew that what he was doing was wrong. And the men screamed and cried for their families—Oswald was right there with them, trying to comfort them. He was sorry, but he could not let them go. Not then. *Not ever*. After all, they would surely call the police, and he would go to jail.

Why? Anyone would ask. Why succumb to the route of such an atypical, capturer lifestyle?

Because.

That's the only explanation Oswald could ever give to himself. He feels the rush whenever he comes across an officer, or someone knocks on his door saying they heard screaming. He was invincible, on top of the world. On the pinnacle of exhilaration. He gets hard just thinking about it. If not for their kidnapping, the three would be friends in another lifetime. Paul and Krin thought he was a nice guy, and that's what was "off" about him.

Day Two

"It's gotta be morning," Krin guesses, trying to play night or day. He goes on about last week's news.

Paul stares at the two large vats of grain and water. "How many gallons, do ya' think?"

Krin stares at the vats. "That's a good barrel size. Maybe fifty gallons?"

"Why would he leave us barrels of food and water?" Paul thinks aloud. *Why?* he repeats in his mind.

Krin shrugs and plays in the water with his hands.

"Krin," Paul says, worried. "I think you should stop that."

Krin obeys his friend's command.

"I don't think he's coming back," Paul adds, his eyes widening with the realization.

Krin turns serious.

"I think he left us," Paul whispers.

The two men do nothing except stare at the barrels and slowly comprehend their fates.

"Maybe he's gone on vacation? I don't think he would just leave us," Krin says as if trying to conjure hope.

Paul shakes his head.

"Let's say a couple of days. Maybe a week. He'll be back," Krin remarks. "He'll be back."

Krin rubs his knees. Paul knows the healing scars itch. He gently touches his own stitches, pondering the water they had wasted playing splash together.

Day Seven

The waste bucket overflows with sewage. Paul tries to toss the waste as far as he can toward their discarded, now decomposed legs, lying in the corner of the room. He picks up the bucket and, with one motion, pitches the contents. The mess flings across the floor and lands in a splatter. The upside? The mess is away from them, and they can use their waste bucket again.

Paul gulps water into his mouth and spits it over his hands, creating a steady stream he could use to wash his hands.

"Okay," Paul says, taking charge. "We need this grain and water to last as long as possible. At least until . . ." he trails off. "Jesus! What if we are *really* abandoned?"

Krin barges in. "Well, you deal with food and I'll—" He yanks at his chains and digs at the concrete where it is made solid into the wall. "—try to break free from these chains."

"Four handfuls a day should do us good. Maybe . . . three seconds of drinking after every meal. How does that sound?" Paul asks.

"It's a plan," Krin says, struggling against metal that will not budge. His wrist is raw and, his nails are chipped from meddling at the concrete. The thought of reuniting with his wife keeps him digging at the thing.

He imagines escaping and his wife greeting him. She'll probably have a knitted scarf ready for him to wear. Warm, made with love, and very itchy. She'll talk all day about her newest board game campaign and the character she embodied. And he would listen, glancing at her thin, cracked lips and smiling to himself. The thought of the two embracing under the ugliest quilt, flashlight in hand, reading ridiculously long fantasy novels, or watching pirated action movies on his phone screen, made him smile.

How is she now? he asked himself. *Is she mourning and crying over me? Or has she found some dashing, charming man who could dress up as fantasy characters with her? Maybe someone who could give her that child she so yearned for.*

But what if she waits for me? Would she look at my now double-amputated body differently? Her library gig alone can barely pay for our New England apartment. I'll need a wheelchair, a new accessible interior for my home, and all sorts of therapy. Face tightening, eyes watering, and body tensing, he yanks on his chains. His rage fills the room, reverberating with each *clink* and *clank*.

He is helpless.

Day Fourteen

Paul takes a careful handful of grain into his mouth. He chews with a disgusted face, each crunch elongated and exaggerated. Three big gulps of water washed the food down. Krin's handful is next. After taking the grain into his palms, Krin consumes small bites to find or savor some pleasant taste. He imagines it to be popcorn—buttery and salty—but that makes the bland handful even duller. ·

They assume their meal to be breakfast. Maybe it is morning outside. They wait hours until Paul suggests that maybe it is afternoon and time to take another handful. The single bulb dangling from the ceiling flickers. It blinks away, saying its last goodbye to the chained men. And then, they are in the darkness, surrounded by the smell of bodily waste and decaying limbs.

"At least I'm not alone," Krin says, smiling through the darkness.

Paul does not respond, and Krin suspects Paul is already asleep.

Later, Paul awakens to the sound of Krin munching on grain.

"Hey!" Paul yells. "Hey, what are you doing?!"

Krin shrugs his shoulders with a surprised, helpless, and confused glance. Even so, in the grips of rage, Paul tackles him.

"How many handfuls did you take?"

"Just one, man. Easy!"

Paul punches Krin in the face. "Don't lie to me."

"Just one. I swear."

Paul lifts himself off a tearful Krin then turns his back to him.

Day Thirty

Krin makes sure that Paul is awake to eat his first meal of the day. They've kept rats from feasting on their barrels, but that still does not stop the rodents from fervently trying. The men's once-clean clothes are now filthy. Pants hang loose from their waists, and shirts drape over their shoulders. There is nothing to do but sleep. Sleep and talk.

Krin talks on and on about his wonderful wife, his wonderful nerdy hobbies, his wonderful job at a comic book shop—everything more wonderful than the last.

Paul isn't jealous; he just wishes people like Krin would ditch their fantasy lands. Paul rarely spoke about his life. Why would he? Nothing is fun about the past of a former addict, deadbeat dad, and trailer-park recluse. If he gets out . . . *when* he gets out, he will do a line or two. That's it. Just two. A celebration of life. A reward of resilience.

His body, feeling only skin and bone, reminded him of the body he used to have: all skin and bones. His clothes used to fit him just like this, baggy and sagging. He imagines there are tons of posters and pictures on the backs of milk cartons searching for Krin. But for him? A felon? Who'd give a rat's ass about him other than the landlord for his money?

"Our supply is getting low. We should probably cut back a little," says Paul with his nose above the water barrel. He puts his hand inside to measure the depth. "Have you found a weak point in your chains?"

"Nothing yet," Krin replies.

Paul scratches and pats at the stitches on his knees. They hurt now. The light buzzes and turns back on, but dim Paul blinks rapidly, adjusting to the light, then gets a look at his stitched knees. They are colored purple and blue. The veins in his arms peek blue through the skin.

"Paul."

"What's that?" he answers.

"Nothing. I didn't say anything," Krin says, lifting his head.

Day Sixty

A half-tailed rat scurries across Krin's thighs. The little rodents no longer fear the men chained in their domain, and Krin doesn't bother shooing this broken-tailed critter away. The two men have become decorations to the little crawlies.

"I'm gonna call you Buddy." Krin picks up the half-tailed rat and watches as the tiny creature jumps on its hind legs and twirls.

Paul slides his finger against the bottom of the barrel, taking the last handful of grain. The water barrel still has a few gulps left. "You wanna split this?"

Krin eagerly puts his hands out and palms up. His stomach is sunken and aches. To the best of his ability, Paul pours half a handful into the other's hands. Krin feels the weight of his portion, and is dissatisfied. "That's not half."

"Yes, it is," Paul says.

"Look at your portion. That's way more."

The two bicker until Krin lunges at Paul (partially as payback for the punch Paul had given him months ago).

The grain spreads into the air and falls to the ground like heavy rain. The two men say nothing to each other and fall asleep stomachs empty. All the food is gone.

"Krin." Paul shakes Krin awake and points to the corner. "Krin, he's right there." Paul shakes him again.

"There's no one over there. We're alone here."

"No, he's been watching us the entire time."

Krin leans toward the corner of the room, opening his eyes as wide as possible. "There's no one—"

"Look harder."

Fancying, Krins continues his stare. Could there possibly be eyes peering through holes in the concrete? He can see it now. Yes! Someone watching. "I see it," Krin says.

"He watches us," Paul whispers.

Day Sixty-Seven

Buddy, the half-tailed rat, sits atop the empty water barrel, *eek*-ing with his new friend Krin.

"How are ya?" Krin says into the dark.

The animal replies with a squeak that only Krin can understand.

"How's the family?"

He converses through grumbles of his stomach and his slowing heartbeats. He itches and picks at his knees. Krin feels the scars healed over the stitches. Through the dingy light, he sees his legs are a burnt-red color. Krin also sees Paul slumped against the wall seemingly listening to him talk to Buddy.

"I had a family once," Paul interrupts in a low voice. "I had a girl. My baby girl. Taken away from me." Paul's voice quivers. "A wife. A house." He breaks, and the tears come in droves. "I wasted it all. I wasted it all to get high."

Krin puts his arm around him with a love that no one else will ever have for two men in a basement. Together. Alone. Paul ugly cries now, his mouth downturned and his voice nearly unrecognizable. He remembers the first time he did PCP. He was in middle school. Mom and Dad had been fighting—no, not arguing—fist-fighting.

After his first hit, he was on top of the world. He could fly. He could see his childhood home and the dingy street it was on. All the colors were vibrant instead of the dull gray they had become in his life. His first destination: the clouds. They were as soft as holding a baby bunny in his hands.

He'd never forget that first high, trying repeatedly to get back to it. Recapture that feeling. But every time after that, he just got lower and lower to the ground until he was in a hole, lying there stuck. Jumping and screaming for help in a dark abyss. That's when the wife left with his baby girl—he didn't blame her. He couldn't blame her. He would've left himself too.

Paul cries on Krin's shoulder, and, for the day, they ignore their rumbling stomachs.

Day Seventy

Paul hears a scratching rat and entices the little rodent to his feet. "C'mere. C'mere little fella."

Wham!

He stomps on the rodent, flattening him. Starving, he eats the insides except for the brains and the intestines. Paul glances at Krin who is holding Buddy tight. The rodent squeaks and nudges its nose. Paul's stomach rumbles again. He can't take it anymore. He bolts for Buddy, snatching it from Krin's hands and biting its head off in one swipe.

"Buddy!" Krin cries. He thrashes at Paul but his strength fails him. "Buddy . . ." Krin whimpers and slumps down.

Paul sleeps after his meal, leaving Krin friendless. Krin leans forward and takes a whiff of Paul. His hunger is hard, and he licks his lips.

Day Seventy-One

Krin squeezes out whatever excrement he has in his body. He searches through it to find any remnants still suitable to re-eat. A bug crawls on the wall. Krin smashes it fast and chews it.

The men both pant. Their stitches are itchy. They can feel the bubbling of the scars.

"Krin," A whisper comes from the walls: a feminine voice, a familiar voice.

It's Jean! Krin's heart flickers.

Silence.

"Krin," the whispers continue.

Krin closes his eyes and ignores it, knowing the voice to be a figment of his mind. That night he dreams of playing video games with his wife in their apartment.

Day Seventy-Two

Paul faces the corner. He sees it now. A set of eyes peering through the gray concrete wall. A set of wild eyes.

"Dad?" The eyes seem to speak. "Dad?" A little girl's voice.

"That's my baby." Paul crawls toward the eyes until the chain's length prevents further movement.

"Dad?"

"Cara, it's me, your dad."

"Dad?"

Paul whimpers, "Cara?"

For several minutes, the exchange continues. The eyes keep questioning, "Dad?"

Paul's voice gets louder with each response until he gives up. He stays awake, hearing his baby call him "Dad?"

Day Seventy-Three

The two men are strewn about on the cold floors, their food and water exhausted. Their scars lift and peel, making it hurt to scratch. Krin turns toward a snoring Paul, whose clothes are loose on his body as Krin's are on him. They've ignored the smell of the thrown excrement and bony, decomposed leg limbs. The men can feel their veins through their stretchy skin.

Krin leans closer to Paul to feel the man's sleeping breath against his cheeks. He climbs atop the unsuspecting man and licks his face.

Paul awakens to an unwanted wetness. "What the hell?" He punches Krin with all the force he has.

Krin throws himself on Paul again, this time biting his ear. The ear is partially severed, and he tastes blood as it seeps from the wound. With the ear in his mouth, Krin chews. It is the first time in months that he has eaten meat.

Paul, the stronger of the two, slams Krin against the wall. He slams him again. This time, he hears a crack and Krin groans. The third slam, Krin is unconscious as the back of his head splits against the wall. After the fourth slam, Paul is sure the man, once a friend, has died.

He places his friend on the ground, wipes the blood off his face, and gazes upon his red hands. Cautiously, he brings his fingers to his nose to sniff the blood. The smell reminds him of walking through the deli section of a grocery store. Packages of raw meat entice his mind. He brings his fingers to his mouth, closes his eyes, and

licks the bloody fingers. He caresses Krin's lifeless body.
His stomach moans again.

Paul is hungry.

Day Seventy-Four

**A Boston man was arrested and charged with
the kidnapping, torture, and death of seven
individuals over ten years. Oswald Mendle-
ton, a white male, was found by Boston authorities in a hidden cabin in Boston Harbor
Islands State Park. Police officers raided his
late home, which had been for sale for several
months. Authorities say they got an anony-
mous tip after someone reported screaming
from beneath the house. Officers said they
found one survivor at the scene. No further
details have been released—our sympathies
to the families and loved ones of the victims.**

YOUR NECK SMELLS OF SALT

Your neck smells of salt—
   anchovies
   May I . . .
   have a taste?

LICKING

His body melds with hers: rhythmic thumps and groans and moans of pleasure. Eyes shut and mouth agape, she whimpers. Sweat rolls down their bodies.

Faster.

His skin ripples and then tightens. She clenches her teeth and curves her back like an alley cat daring someone to touch it.

"Mara," he whispers before collapsing, his weight crushing her thin self.

She lies there in post-orgasm bliss. There's a sound, but she cannot comprehend it.

"Mara," her husband murmurs. "Mara, the phone."

"You get it," she whispers.

"It's probably the shop."

He's probably right. She picks up the phone. "'Ello," she answers with a plastic English accent. "Mink?!"

Mara turns to her husband. "Mink! My first mink. I have to go. Now."

"Hon, you said—"

"My first mink!" She jumps out of bed and rushes to the bathroom, deciding on a polka-dotted dress to match her personality. Her crystal blue eyes and messy hair reflect back in the mirror—she'll take a hot curler to it once her shower is done. Before stepping into the shower, the overflowing trash can catches her attention. The mess is odd for the otherwise spotless bathroom. The ovulation strips, the fertility kits, and countless negative pregnancy tests taunt her. *Don't think about it*, she says to herself.

The Classy Lady is pink. Blinding pink. A humble shop for an ambitious seamstress. A chandelier, fit for the Ritz if it weren't plastic, hangs from the ceiling in the waiting area. The mirrors are adorned with golden trims, and the carpet is a dazzling lemon yellow. The bell hanging above the front door chimes.

"Jeanie!" Mara yells, hurrying to the back of the shop. "Jeanie, where—?"

A silver-haired woman wearing cat-eye glasses stands with a calm smile, holding a mink coat.

"Bona fide. It's the real thing," Jeanie says, her hands and body quivering from a precondition. Her age showed, but goddammit, she could still sew like no one's business.

The two women stare at each other in awe as if seeing the future in each other's eyes. Jeanie breaks the stare with a giggle, and the two jump up and down in glee. Or, at least, Mara jumps and Jeanie slightly bends her fragile knees.

Mara gets working on the coat. She inspects the seams and runs her fingers down the soft fur. *Poor animal,* she thinks to herself. For such a beautiful thing, it's an ugly process—a death necessary to birth a beauty. Besides a tiny rip where it drapes over the left shoulder, the coat is in fine condition.

With a face of focus, Mara gets to work, determined to finish the project earlier than expected. Hours pass. She is careful at sewing, making sure not to cause damage to the expensive piece. The doorbell rings. Her head jolts up to see her husband approaching the backroom. She sends him a smile, which he returns. He knocks on the wall as if to say, "You ready?"

"Here to distract me?" Mara asks.

He leans against the wall with a brown paper bag dangling at his side. She trots to him, kisses his full and slicked lips, then tightly embraces him. But curiosity overcomes her.

"What's in the bag?" she asks, still holding onto him.

He reaches into the bag and pushes a bouquet before her face. "For madam," he says. "Can I steal you for a moment?" Albert breathes in Mara's ear, making the hair on her neck stand up.

"Lunch?" she asks, coy and bashful.

"You know me so well." He kisses her thin, red lips then uses a handkerchief to wipe the lipstick off his mouth.

Holding hands, the two exit the store and walk down the pavement. Cornelia is a perfect town. Everyone knows one another by their first name and can recite each other's family tree by heart. All the homes have the same pastel template and layout. Folks often leave their doors unlocked as crime in Cornelia is rare, or at least, town police stalk the wrong sorts until they can't stand it. And by the "wrong sorts," that meant Blacks, Jews, and single mothers. Nuclear is the only acceptance here. It was almost eerie, the sameness of everything.

The two stroll through the posh town holding hands, nearing their favorite cafe, The Busy Bee. They enter, and Mara sighs in delight at the sight. Toddlers playing hide-n-seek beneath a table, a man at a computer working, two teens on an early afternoon date, and the aroma of freshly buttered croissants, sesame seed bagels, and hot coffee.

In the corner of the café is an unusual sight. A woman wearing chunky gold bangles and layers of colorful sarongs sits at a round table. Her face is smooth and beautiful, but her hands are wrinkled and old. A sign at the table reads, "Tarot readings, five dollars."

Despite being a Christian woman who didn't dabble in occult matters, Mara is curious. The woman must be from that new metaphysical shop Agrippa. Mara's religion, though, does not stop her from sitting at the tarot woman's table.

"Five dollars," says the woman. Her heavy Romani accent is darkly sensual, as is her face. She reaches out her hand, expecting money to be placed in it. Mara pays her.

"What do you wish to know?"

Mara hasn't thought that far, but one question bounces into her mind. She glances at her husband, who is busy ordering with the cashier.

"My love life," she whispers.

With a toothy smile, the woman shuffles her cards, chants words that Mara cannot understand, and slams the deck before Mara and points to it. "Cut it."

Mara picks up the upper half of the deck and places it under the lower half, switching the top and bottom. Then, the Romani woman spreads the cards on the table in a face-down fan shape. "Choose three. See your future."

Mara decides on the three cards that will show her future. The woman then takes them and flips them, one by one, placing them in front of Mara.

"The Devil," the woman chuckles. "The Lovers." Then, the third card. "The Empress."

The face cards are bent and damaged, showing their age and frequent use. The Devil reveals a horned-goat figure perched atop a throne with a naked man and woman at either side with a chain around their necks. The Lovers card also shows a naked man and woman. They look up at an angelic figure in the sky. Their arms are open as if about to receive something. And the Empress card displays a regal woman wearing a golden crown, sitting leisurely on her throne.

The woman's chuckles evolve into a belly laugh. Mara tilts her head, trying to gain meaning from the cards. She leans in and asks the woman, "*What*? What do you see?"

The woman continues to laugh.

"What is it?" Mara demands.

"Power," replies the woman. "I see power in your love life. The ultimate power."

Mara hesitates to ask a question she has been dying to ask.

"Let it out," the woman says as if she had read her mind.

"Will I . . . will I finally have a child?" Mara asks.

The woman laughs again this time choking through the laughter. "Yes." She reaches her hand out. "Tip?"

Mara lays a dollar bill in her hand. The woman frowns but stuffs it into the fabric fold around her waist. "Come see me at Agrippa down the street if you wish for more."

Don't count on it, Mara thinks while walking away to meet her husband. He's already sitting at a table and halfway through a BLT sandwich.

"What's your fortune?" her husband asks, mocking the situation.

"She said we're gonna have a baby."

"A baby, huh?" Her husband raises his eyebrows.

A baby! Wouldn't that be something? she thinks.

They continue their lunch at the café, laughing together and filling their bellies with overpriced pastries.

Glancing at her watch, Mara says, "Oh, I must return to the shop." She stands and cleans up the mess of crumbs she made.

Albert holds her hand, begging her not to go.

"Oh, I must."

"I've got work to do at the office anyways," he says, giving in.

He leaves a sizable tip on the table and then kisses on his wife's lips. They go their separate ways.

Mara returns to the shop, where a familiar face waits in the front lobby.

"She said she wanted you only," Jeanie whispers to Mara, peeking back at the woman with long hair and a sleek figure. It's the woman. The tarot card reader. Her fingers are intertwined and her face is worried.

"Hello—" Mara hesitates. "Well, I didn't catch your name from before."

"Ioana," the woman replies.

"What can I do for you?" Mara walks to the backroom and fiddles with fabrics and supplies.

Ioana raises her voice so Mara can hear from the backroom. "I did not come for your services. I came to warn you."

"Warn me?" Mara pokes her head from the backroom, curious. "About what?"

"The baby."

Mara scoffs and continues with her busy work.

"You must not have the baby," Ioana continues.

"My husband and I have been trying for years. I'd love to have a little one."

"When you left, I pulled more cards. I saw death reincarnate. I saw his eyes." Ioana makes a claw with her hands and motions as if being strangled. "His hands were gripping your neck . . . I saw—"

"Miss." Mara emerges from the backroom and approaches the woman. "Thank you, but I don't believe in that superstitious stuff. I'm a Christian woman."

Mara returns to the backroom, and the woman tries to follow, but Jeanie blocks access.

"Employees only," Jeanie says, standing tall.

"Please, listen to me. You must not have the baby."

"Ma'am, I'm going to ask you to leave now," Jeanie declares.

Ioana surrenders and lifts her hands in the air like she's held at gunpoint. "If you need me, I am down the street. Agrippa."

The woman leaves a royal purple business card on the front desk as Jeanie motions for her to exit. Ioana obeys, giving one last glance at the place before leaving.

"Folks are getting weirder and weirder by the day," says Jeanie, returning to her work.

Mara says nothing as she fumbles with the large mink in her hands.

The day is over, and evening is upon the town. Mara walks home as she always does. Even though she doesn't want to take it seriously, she ponders what Ioana said. *Am I in danger?* And what about the baby she has longed for? She shakes her head and lets the thoughts evaporate out of her mind. She has a wonderful husband waiting for her.

The front door to the home is unlocked. She cracks open the door and steps carefully into the foyer.

"Honey?" she calls.

No reply. There is a trail of roses on the floor. She smiles to herself and giggles. Her whole body tingles. She follows the rose petals up the stairs to the master bedroom, enters, and sees her husband, who is in his underwear and has a rose in his mouth. Mara lets out a laugh at the sight. Her husband joins in.

"You wanna try tonight?"

She nods, jumps onto the bed, and plants a horde of kisses on her husband's face. Kneeling on the bed, she does a striptease dance.

"Mara," Albert says, embracing her, feeling her soft places.

She moans, inviting his touch and he kisses her. Their tongues dance with one another as Mara slides her husband's boxes off. He pulls off her clothing, pushes inside her, and the love-making commences.

Hisssss.

Mara's body jerks.

"What's wrong?" Albert asks.

"Nothing, keep going."

He cautiously continues, kissing her neck.

Hisssss.

Mara hears it again but is determined. "Faster," she demands.

His movements are faster now—as fast as he can go.

"Faster," Mara says again, squirming in pleasure.

"Honey, I can't—"

"Faster!" Mara raises her voice, wanting to reach ecstasy.

Albert makes one last attempt at reaching an enjoyable speed for his wife, but he climaxes.

"Faster." She doesn't notice Albert's tiredness.

"Honey, I-I'm finished."

Disappointed, she lifts herself from the bed and heads to the bathroom, slamming the door behind her.

"Honey, I'm sorry," Albert yells to console her.

Mara stares at herself in the mirror upon her nakedness. She is covered in sweat that is not hers. Her hair is wild, and her eyes . . . the irises of her eyes are a bright red.

Hissss.

"Albert!" She runs out of the bathroom to her husband. "What color are my eyes?"

"Beautiful blue, darling."

"Are you sure?"

"Of course, honey."

She hurries back to the bathroom and glances in the mirror again. The once red eyes are now bright blue. *I'm going crazy. A shower will straighten me up.*

Mara lets steaming water run over her, washing the sweat and remnants of love-making off her body. The shower is not as inviting as it usually is. Her head throbs under the water, but not as much as between her legs. She was not satisfied tonight. She goes to touch herself then pulls away. *No, I must sleep.* After a short time in the shower, Mara prepares for bed.

"I love you." Albert gives her a goodnight kiss, which she is not anxious to receive.

Within minutes, he is sound asleep, yet she is awake, tracing the stucco lines of the ceiling in her mind.

Hisssss.

Mara throws the covers over her head and forces herself to sleep. A set of red eyes peering from the darkness invades her dreams.

Hissss Hu-man Wo-man Sk-in So Soft Neck So Sup-ple Grace-ful, the creature from the darkness says.

Her body shivers.

The dimly lit vicious smile invades the darkness. *I Want . . . I Want You*, it says.

She tosses and turns in bed.

Out comes its tongue. *Licking . . . Licking . . . Licking . . .*

The pain turns into fulfillment and she moans.

Tasty.

Then, the thin smile disappears into the shadows.

It is morning, and Albert has already gone to the office. Mara shifts, feeling a wetness between her legs. *Wet dream, huh?* After putting on a dress covered in pink tulips and making herself breakfast, Mara heads to The Classy Lady. Jeanie is there waiting for her.

"Any news?" Mara asks, entering the shop.

"Just the usual. Rips and holes."

"Great!"

Mara enters the backroom and sits down at her sewing table. The mink waits. She's had the thing for days now. It is time to finish it. She takes the mink and feels its softness. Inspecting it, she runs her fingers over what's left of the hole she has to mend. *Poor mink.* She threads the needle and begins her tedious sewing on the expensive piece.

Finding her work entrancing, Mara stares at the stitches. *Last night,* she thinks. *Last night.* She remembers the hissing noise and that cruel smile in the darkness.

"Mara."

The hurt she felt in her dream, followed by intense satisfaction—she yearned for it. Itched for it.

"Mara."

Her legs quiver. She closes her eyes, waiting for that oh-so-good feeling. Whatever it is, she wants more.

"Mara!" Jeanie shakes Mara, who is dazed. "Mara, look!"

Mara holds up her bleeding red finger. Her needle has pierced through the index. A lovely satin stitch through the top layer of skin. She jumps out of her seat and yelps, and an electric pain rushes from her fingers to her belly, which now hurts more than her fingers—as if a knife was making a mess of her insides. Mara doubles over, crying out.

Jeanie beckons her to sit down. "I'll call an ambulance," Jeanie says, reaching for the phone.

"No!" Mara utters through the throbbing pain. "I'll have my husband drive me to the doctor."

She gags and groans as she dials his office. Meanwhile, Jeanie stops the bleeding from Mara's sewn finger with bandages from the first aid kit. Holding her twisting stomach, Mara hears her husband burst through the store doors. He lifts Mara, carries her to the car, places her in the back seat, and drives straight to their family doctor.

"Welp." Dr. Minshaw is a short, stout man hiding his balding head with a poorly done comb-over. He finishes re-bandaging Mara's index finger. "It seems, Mrs. Miller, that you are pregnant."

Mara covers her mouth with her hand. Her husband throws his arms around her, practically jumping on her.

"Pregnant," she says, barely getting the word out. "I'm pregnant?"

After years of trying, endless tears, and those sad days thinking she was less of a woman, she is finally with child.

"I'm prescribing you something for the pain. If it continues, see me immediately. Hmm?"

"Oh, yes, sir!"

Mara goes home and relaxes for the rest of the day. Albert takes the day off and spends time with his wife and his child-to-be. They lie in bed; Mara is in her husband's arms, spooning in bed.

Whack!

Mara pulls back, realizing she has just slapped her husband's hand away. "Oh! I don't know what's gotten into me."

She takes his hand and places it on her belly. Carefully, he caresses. Mara wonders what her stomach will feel like in a few weeks—months. She closes her eyes and envisions the face of her unborn baby. The image in her mind is unfocused. She thinks harder, and the thought comes into view.

Red eyes.

Months pass. Mara's stomach overcomes her tiny body. She feels like she is lugging a wiggling watermelon in her womb. Dr. Minshaw continues to see her for belly pain, which seems to be relentless. She is always in pain—her lower back, feet, and stomach. Carrying a baby is not what she imagined it to be.

To Mara's surprise, she grows increasingly territorial over her stomach, not allowing anyone, including her husband, to pet her baby bump. She smacks away prying hands more than a few times, followed by an immediate apology. She does not know why she feels so possessive over her little one.

And poor Albert. Mara thwarts his attempts at intimacy. She winces at his good morning kisses and afternoon embraces. She notices he doesn't wake up with a smile anymore. Work becomes his priority and, in some ways, she's sure, his solace from home. Maybe things will return to normal after she has the baby.

Mara lies on the examination table with a cold jelly on her stomach. She squirms at the touch of the doctor's latex glove on her bare belly—she wants to bite that hand off. Sweat drips down her forehead as the transducer probe glides across her body. *Don't touch my baby.* Her jaw clenches, and she grinds her teeth until they hurt. *What is happening to me*? She exhales a long breath, trying to steady her heartbeat.

"Just relax," Dr. Minshaw says in a quiet voice. "And there it is."

Minshaw points to the monitor, circling the head of the black-and-white lump on the screen.

"Can we know the sex?"

"Let's see . . ." Minshaw guides the probe and squints at the screen. "It's a . . ." Minshaw does a double-take and blinks. "We should be able to see the sex by now," he mumbles.

"Is everything alright?" Albert asks.

Mara lifts her head to get a glimpse of the screen.

"Well, let's say the sex is undetermined right now," he says, turning off the machine. "Your baby seems healthy. I'm not sure why you're still having stomach pains. I may send you to a specialist."

Mara shakes her head, denying the request. She glances down at her large belly and cringes at the thought of another doctor touching her child. "No, I'm fine. Really."

Albert insists. "Honey, are you sure?"

"I said I'm fine!" Mara declares in a stern tone—one she's never used with Albert.

The two drive home in unbearable silence. Mara is calm but feels Albert's eyes scanning her. When they get home, Mara hurries up the stairs to the bedroom, slams the door behind her, and locks it, leaving her husband behind.

"Mara." Albert knocks. "Mara, are you okay?"

"Yes," she replies before plopping onto the bed and covering her face.

"Can I do anything?"

"I said I'm fine!" she snaps.

After hearing Albert descend the stairs, Mara lets the tears flow. *What's wrong with me?* she thinks to herself. She holds her belly, and a wave of relief fills her. It's almost as if someone is whispering in her ear.

Everything's going to be alright. Trust me. Trust me. Tr-ust M-e

A growling, unlike that from hunger, more like a low animal snarl causes Mara to jolt up. She searches for the source but finds nothing. And her stomach pulsates and hurts. The pain is hard. Then again, a growl. Mara looks down. The threatening growl . . . is coming from inside her!

Mara cries out, holding her stomach. *There's a monster inside me*! Covering her hands with her mouth, she prevents herself from gagging. A scratching comes from inside her body. She shuffles to the bathroom, lifts her shirt, and gazes in the mirror. There's a weird blurriness, and then, as if it is coming through her skin from the inside, a strange symbol appears on her belly.

"Oh, God!" she shouts, touching the skin. *This can't be real*, she thinks. *My God, what is going on*? At once, the sound of Ioana's name floats through her mind. She can hear the woman's voice telling her not to have the baby. *What were those three cards again*? *The Devil*, *The Lovers*, *The Empress*? Mara checks the wall clock. Maybe she should see that woman, the tarot reader. She neatens her attire and prepares for a swift journey to the occult shop.

Walking into Agrippa, Mara's eyes adjust to the dark interior of the store, decorated with animal skulls, colorful tapestries, and tarot cards hanging by threads. Smokey incense is lit, making her eyes burn and water. Despite the plentiful products, the store lacks customers.

"Excuse me." Mara approaches the cashier at the front desk. "I'm looking for Ioana."

The lady cashier, her loving smile invites, points to a backroom hidden behind purple velvet curtains. A sign in front says, "Fortunes, Five Dollars."

Mara slips through the velvet curtains and sees Ioana at a table, intensely gazing into a large obsidian ball.

"Ioana?"

The woman looks up from her trance. "Ah, the seamstress!"

"I need your . . . assistance."

The woman reaches out her hand and motions her fingers in a gimme fashion. "Five dollars."

Mara rummages through her purse and pulls out a crumpled five-dollar bill.

"I see that you're having the baby," says Ioana, peeking at Mara's belly.

"I've been feeling weird lately."

"Weird. How?"

Mara lifts her shirt to show the etched symbol on her skin. The woman jumps from her seat and backs into the wall. She grabs a stick of incense from a stash underneath the table, lights it, and mumbles words Mara cannot understand.

"What is it?" Mara asks.

"That is the sigil of *Lilû*."

"Lilû?"

"Yes, a demon who seduces women and . . ." Ioana trails off. She takes a good look at the sigil. ". . . and impregnates them."

Mara blurts out in nervous laughter. "A demon? Having sex with humans?"

Ioana's face is serious. "You must get rid of the baby."

A desire to slap the woman overwhelms Mara. "I am a God-fearing woman! Getting rid of the baby is out of the question. Besides, I've been trying for years to have a child. I won't give up now."

"Well," Ioana says. "I can try to do a cleansing. To save the baby."

"Cleansing?"

"An exorcism."

Mara folds her arms in protest, then recalls the images of red eyes. "Shouldn't an exorcism be done by a priest?"

Ioana laughs. "You watch too many movies."

Mara huffs and finally says, "Okay, let's do it."

Ioana calls for the cashier, who enters the room. "She will help."

Ioana pulls a large box from underneath the table as if pre-prepared for the event. She opens it to expose oils, scraps of paper, homemade paper dolls, ornamental knives, and trinkets. She pulls out a pair of leather straps.

Mara resists. "You're not putting those on me."

"It's for your own protection."

Uncertain, Mara hesitates. The thought of the growling and piercing red eyes comes to her, and she nods. The woman tightens the straps around Mara's arms, securing her to the chair. Ioana and the cashier hold hands and pray. In unison, they say, "We thank the Great Mother. We thank the Great Father. We call upon our spirits, our deities, to protect us. Guide us, oh Great Ones."

Ioana then chants in a language Mara can't decipher while her assistant lays scraps of paper dipped in a strange oil onto her belly. Written on some of the scraps are scriptures that she recognizes from the Bible; she is unsure about the others.

A burning sensation zooms through her. "Um, it's getting hot," Mara utters.

Ioana chants faster.

"No, I mean, it's burning."

Mara's belly is now hot to the touch. She whines and squirms in the chair. Then, she coughs and spits, choking on words she tries to get out.

Ioana chants faster.

The lights flicker, and the assistant joins in.

Mara cries out, "I'm on fire inside!"

Her belly lets out a low snarl. Ioana places her hand on the stomach. Together, she and the assistant shout their prayer. The low snarl turns into a sickening gurgling.

Mara struggles to keep conscious as she feels an unnatural movement coming from inside her belly. She lets out a rippling scream at the sight. The skin visibly stretches as whatever is on the inside moves and shifts.

The lights sputter again, then burst, getting pieces of glass bulb into Ioana's eyes. Even so, she closes her bloody eyes and continues with her chant. The chair wobbles and shakes, then lifts. Soon, it floats.

Ioana and the assistant pray louder. The chair floats higher, and Mara's head feels close to the ceiling.

"I command you out!" Ioana declares.

The wooden chair slams to the ground, breaking and letting Mara loose. She feels a burning in her eyes and redness clouds her vision. Ioana and her assistant cease their chants. A cruel silence happens upon them. Mara, now on the ground, stares at the ceiling with a look of horror. Her mouth is stretched open and twitching.

"Mara?" Ioana inches toward her. "Mara?"

Mara's focus jolts from the ceiling to Ioana and lets out a low growl.

"Oh no," Ioana says.

Mara dashes toward Ioana, taking her by the neck with seemingly superhuman strength. The assistant comes from behind, trying to pry Mara off the fortune teller. With one hand swipe, Mara pushes the woman away with formidable power. The assistant flies into cabinets with herb-filled mason jars and knick-knacks. She lands with a *crack*, breaking her back and neck vertebrae—a deadly force.

Mara continues choking Ioana, who gasps as her eyes become laced with red. She watches as the life leaves her slumping body. Ioana is still, her arms drop to her sides. Fluids escape her body, signifying that she is indeed dead.

Mara is alone . . . alive. Growling at the sight of the bodies. A sharp pain ripples through her. She lets out a terrible scream and falls to the ground. A gush of liquid flows from between her legs. She screams again, this time the pain coming from her dilating uterus.

It's time.

She takes off her bottoms and pushes. Immense pressure crushes her tiny body. Her screams echo through the empty store with no one to help. The head crowns, Mara's eyes roll in the back of her head at the pain, and she howls.

"Help me!" she says in a voice that is not hers.

The baby is halfway out. Mara's breaths are rapid as blood flows from her body onto the floor. She pushes again. The legs and feet come out. The baby shrieks upon its first breath of life. Mara embraces the newborn and sings a lullaby to soothe its crying.

"My baby," she whispers in its ear.

A low growl reverberates through the room, and she plants a kiss on its wet, slimy, and bloody forehead. A beautiful baby boy. With deep red eyes.

I LICKED YOU

I licked you so softly. I wanted you to feel my wetness against your skin. I licked you hungrily. I wanted to taste the follicles and dirt on your flesh. Let me nibble and bite. Let it tickle and make you giggle. I licked you so I could ingest your goody essence.

Printed in the USA
CPSIA information can be obtained
at www.ICGtesting.com
LVHW090618080224
771185LV00054B/1510

9 798989 624201